Busytown Mysteries™

With the timeless characters of RICHARD SCARRY

The Missing Apple Mystery

adapted by Ellie Seiss
based on the screenplay "The Big Apple Mystery"
written by Bob Ardiel

Simon Spotlight
New York London Toronto Sydney

SIMON SPOTLIGHT
An imprint of Simon & Schuster Children's Publishing Division
1230 Avenue of the Americas, New York, New York 10020
Busytown Mysteries™ and all related and associated trademarks are owned by Cookie Jar Entertainment Inc. and
used under license from Cookie Jar Entertainment Inc. © 2010 Cookie Jar Entertainment Inc. All Rights Reserved.
All rights reserved, including the right of reproduction in whole or in part in any form. SIMON SPOTLIGHT and
colophon are registered trademarks of Simon & Schuster, Inc.
For information about special discounts for bulk purchases, please contact Simon & Schuster Special Sales
at 1-866-506-1949 or business@simonandschuster.com.
Manufactured in the United States of America 1110 LAK
10 9 8 7 6 5 4
ISBN 978-1-4424-0227-0

Huckle Cat and his sister, Sally, lived in Busytown with their friends Lowly Worm, Hilda Hippo, Pig Will, and Pig Won't. They loved everything in their town from the Busytown Park to the bustling Busytown streets.

Huckle, Sally, and Lowly especially loved peeking through the fence and watching everything going on at the Busytown construction site.

"This must be the busiest place in Busytown!" said Lowly.

"I know!" Huckle agreed. "It's hard to know where to look. I don't want to miss any of the action."

"I see a welder welding . . .

and a digger digging . . .

and even someone operating a really tall crane!" said Sally.

Just then the crane operator accidentally knocked a long piece of steel into the sign above the front door of Mr. Green's grocery store.

"Did you see that?" Sally asked Huckle and Lowly.

"The big apple fell right off the sign," said Huckle. "Come on! We've got to check this out."

Huckle, Sally, and Lowly ran over to Mr. Green, who was looking up at his broken sign.

"Where did the big apple go, Mr. Green?" Sally asked the grocer.

"That's what I'd like to know," replied Mr. Green.

Beep! Beep!

Beep! Beep!

Huckle, Sally, and Lowly recognized that honk! It was Goldbug in his Busytown Action Bug News van.

"Goldbug here, reporting live from Hillside Street, where a big apple has just fallen from the sky."

Goldbug turned to Huckle. "You were one of the first people on the scene. Can you describe what you saw?"

"Yes! I saw everything! The big apple on Mr. Green's sign was hit from behind. It came loose and crashed down to the ground."

"But I don't see it here," said Goldbug. "Where did the big apple go?"

"I'm not sure exactly," said Huckle.

"But you saw *everything*," replied Goldbug.

"Well," Huckle began, "I saw *almost* everything—everything except where the big apple went! That, I don't know, but I do know that it has to be around here somewhere and I am going to solve the Missing Apple Mystery!"

Huckle, Sally, and Lowly ran to their vehicles a few stores down from the grocery, ready to start looking for the big apple sign. There was just one problem—they didn't know where to start!

"Which way should we go, Huckle?" asked Lowly just as Hilda Hippo walked past them, kicking a ball. She gave the ball a big kick and it started rolling down the hill. Then she ran down the hill after it.

"Look," said Huckle, "Hilda's round ball is rolling down the hill."

"And the apple sign is also round," said Lowly.

"So maybe it rolled down the hill too!" exclaimed Huckle. "That's the direction we have to start looking for the apple sign. Let's get Busytown!"

Lowly, Huckle, and Sally drove down the hill, keeping a lookout for the apple sign. At the bottom of the hill they spotted Mr. Gronkle with his grocery cart. Mr. Gronkle looked very upset. His groceries were spilled all over the road!

"What happened?" asked Huckle.

"My cart was run over," said Mr. Gronkle. "That's what happened. A big red round thing ran over it."

"Big?" asked Sally.

"Red?" asked Lowly.

"Round?" asked Huckle. "Like a giant wooden apple? Which way did it go?"

Mr. Gronkle scratched his head and thought really hard. "I forget," he said.

Huckle, Lowly, and Sally were all busy thinking about where to go next when they heard someone yelling.

"Hey!" said a man, pointing to Lowly's apple-shaped car. "Which one of you drives that thing?"

"It's mine," said Lowly. "Is something the matter?"

"I'll say there is," said the man. "Next time you want to take a shortcut, don't drive through the flower garden in Town Square. Someone saw a big apple going straight through the tulips!"

"It's the apple sign!" said Huckle. "Thanks, mister! That was just the clue we needed. Come on, team!"

Soon Huckle, Sally, and Lowly reached Town Square.
"Look at the broken fence," said Huckle. "The apple sign must have rolled right over it!"

"And all of the tulips, too!" said Sally.

"Well, at least it's easy to tell where the apple sign was rolling—we just have to follow its trail!" said Huckle.

But before long, Huckle, Sally, and Lowly had come to the end of the apple sign's trail.

"Now how will we figure out which direction to go?" asked Sally.

"The apple sign could have gone any which way," added Lowly.

Huckle wondered aloud. "If I were round, which way would *I* roll?"

"Watch out!" shouted Lowly, pointing to a large wooden spool that was headed their way.

"It's big and round, and it's rolling away!" said Sally.

"Let's follow it," said Huckle. "It'll probably roll to the same place as the apple sign."

Huckle, Sally, and Lowly sped through the streets of Busytown after the runaway spool.

"The spool's headed for Busytown Harbor," said Huckle.

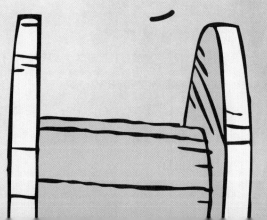

"Splash! Right in the water," said Lowly, as the spool flew off the dock.

"Exactly!" said Huckle. "So that means the apple sign must be in the water too."

Huckle, Sally, and Lowly peered into the water, but didn't see the apple sign.

"Where could it be?" asked Lowly.

Just then Goldbug arrived on the scene looking for an update. "Huckle, what have you and your team discovered so far?"

Huckle frowned. "I thought the apple sign would be here, but it's not."

"Yes it is!" said Sally. "Look—that sailboat was just blocking us from seeing it. Now that the sailboat is moving again, there's the apple sign!"

"Hey! I was right after all!" said Huckle.

"Hurray for Huckle!" Sally and Lowly shouted together.

"But I couldn't have found the missing apple sign without the best team in Busytown," said Huckle.

"Hats off to all of us," said Lowly.

"Well, there you have it, folks," said Goldbug, signing off for the Busytown Action Bug News. "The Missing Apple Mystery has been solved. I'm Goldbug, and that's the *buzz* in Busytown!"